```
E          Sivulich, Sandra
Siv     Stroner
        I'm going on a bear
        hunt
```

| DATE DUE | | |
|---|---|---|
| MAY 1 5 1998 | | |
| MAY 2 0 2002 | | |
| JAN 0 5 2004 | | |
| JAN 0 5 2003 | MAY 1 5 '07 | |
| JAN 2 3 2004 | | |
| | | |
| MAY 1 9 | | |
| | | |

# I'm Going on a Bear Hunt

by Sandra Stroner Sivulich

illustrated by Glen Rounds

E. P. Dutton & Co., Inc. New York

Published simultaneously in Canada by Clarke,
Irwin & Company Limited, Toronto and Vancouver

SBN: 0-525-32535-2   LCC: 72-85257

Typography by Hilda Scott
Printed in the U.S.A.
First Edition

*For Maggie Kimmel, Florence Burmeister,
and the Illinois children's librarians*

I'm going on a bear hunt

*Pound legs like you're walking.*

I'm going on a bear hunt

And I'm not afraid

And I'm not afraid

Goodbye, mother.

Goodbye, mother.

*W*ave.

Off we go through the tall jungle grass

*Hands together sliding—swish sound.*

Now we come to a tall tree.

Maybe if we climb the tree
we'll be able to see better.

*Climb up the tree.*

Hmmm—I don't see anything up here
except birds and leaves.
No bears.

So, we'll slide down the tree.

*Swoosh down.*

Now I come to a big, blue lake.

How'll I get across?

Well, there's only one way.

I'll jump right in and swim across.

*Dive in and do the crawl stroke.*

Now I get to the other side
and shake myself off dry
and . . . oh no!
There is another big, blue lake.

I'm just too tired.

I can only swim across one lake in one day.

How'll I get across?

I guess I'll get into my trusty rowboat

and row across.

*Sing: "Row, row, row your boat."*

Get to the other side and I see a swamp:
an icky swamp, a gooshy swamp,
a muddy, slimey, oozy swamp.

I'll have to walk through all that
ishly mud like this.

*Make slurpy sounds and
make pulling taffy motions.*

Now we get to the other side,
and I still don't see that bear,
but I do see a cave.

I have to get down real low,

and it's dark inside the cave,

and cold.

*Pretend you're crawling—*

*move hands around in a groping manner,*

*and use a very spooky voice.*

And . . .

IT'S A BEAR!!!

*Repeat motions, all in double time.*

**Go through the swamp**

Go through the lake—rowing

Go through the lake—swimming

Climb up the tree

Slide down the tree

Go through the grass

Oh, I'm home at last.

I went on a bear hunt.
I went on a bear hunt.

AND I WASN'T AFRAID.

SANDRA STRONER SIVULICH first heard *I'm Going on a Bear Hunt* when she was telling stories at a children's hospital once a week during graduate school. She "added and subtracted and played with it for years until I had my own variation." She had so many requests from other Illinois children's librarians for copies of her version, she finally decided it might be welcome as a book. Mrs. Sivulich now lives in Erie, Pennsylvania, where she is lecturer in children's literature at Mercyhurst College.

GLEN ROUNDS was born in a sod house in the South Dakota badlands. At different times he has been a cowpuncher, baker, carnival barker, and sign painter. Mr. Rounds studied at the Kansas City Art Institute and the Art Students League in New York City. Mr. Rounds has written and illustrated many books for children; he also illustrated *Contrary Jenkins,* co-authored by Rebecca Caudill and James Ayars. His illustrations for *I'm Going on a Bear Hunt* were done in brush line with shaded pencil overlays for the colors.

The type is set in Bookman. The book was printed by offset at Pearl Pressman Liberty.